I SPY
A SKELETON

For Patrick Finbarr Bowe with a BOO!
and with thanks to Dave and Dan
—J.M.

For Victoria Hamel
—W.W.

Text copyright © 2009 by Jean Marzollo
Cover illustration "Discovery in the Graveyard"
from *I Spy Spooky Night* © 1996 by Walter Wick;
"The Fountain" from *I Spy Spooky Night* © 1996 by Walter Wick;
"Storybook Theater" from *I Spy School Days* © 1995 by Walter Wick;
"Ghost of the Night" from *I Spy Spooky Night* © 1996 by Walter Wick;
"Odds & Ends" from *I Spy* © 1992 by Walter Wick;
"Monster Workshop" from *I Spy Fantasy* © 1994 by Walter Wick;
"Creaky Gate" from *I Spy Spooky Night* © 1996 by Walter Wick;
"The Ghost in the Attic" from *I Spy Mystery* © 1993 by Walter Wick;
"Creepy Crawly Cave" from *I Spy Fun House* © 1993 by Walter Wick;
"Clown Dressing Room" from *I Spy Fun House* © 1993 by Walter Wick;
"The Library" from *I Spy Spooky Night* © 1996 by Walter Wick.

All rights reserved. Published by Scholastic Inc.
SCHOLASTIC, CARTWHEEL BOOKS, and associated logos
are trademarks and/or registered trademarks of Scholastic Inc.
Lexile is a registered trademark of MetaMetrics, Inc.
Library of Congress Cataloging-in-Publication Data

Marzollo, Jean.
I spy a skeleton / by Jean Marzollo ; illustrated by Walter Wick.
p. cm. – (Scholastic reader level 1)
ISBN 978-0-545-17539-5
1. Picture puzzles—Juvenile literature. 2. Skeleton—Juvenile literature. I. Wick, Walter
II. Title. III. Series.
GV1507.P47M292 2009
793.73—dc22   2009024420

ISBN-13: 978-0-545-17539-5
ISBN-10: 0-545-17539-9

10 9 8 7   14 15 16 17

Printed in the U.S.A. • First printing, September 2009   40

I SPY
A SKELETON

Riddles by Jean Marzollo
Photographs by Walter Wick

Cartwheel
·B·O·O·K·S·®

SCHOLASTIC INC.
New York Toronto London Auckland
Sydney Mexico City New Delhi Hong Kong

I spy

a fish,

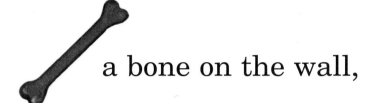 a bone on the wall,

a bat,

and someone about to fall.

I spy

a pumpkin,

 the grin of a cat,

three golden eggs,

and a horn player's hat.

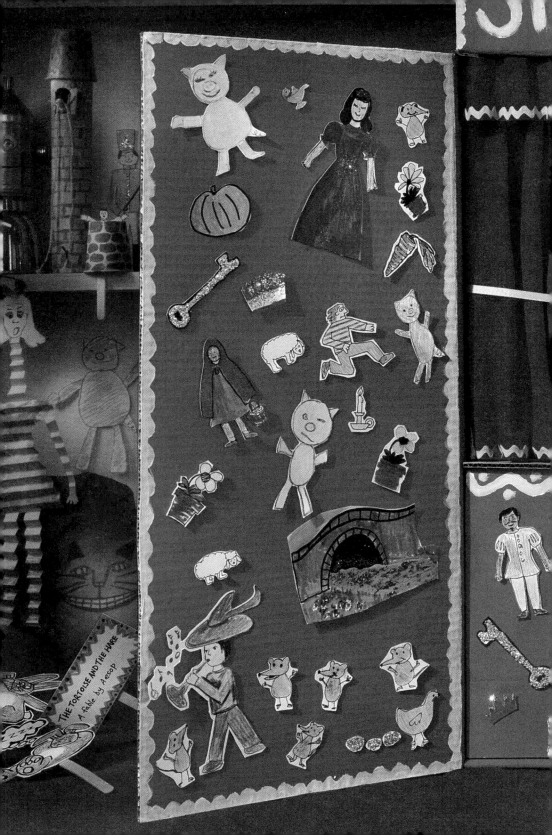

THE TORTOISE AND THE HARE
A fable by Aesop

I spy

a smoky skull,

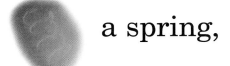 a spring,

a bottle,

a bone,

and a crown for a king.

I spy

 a speedboat,

a silver key,

 a skeleton,

and a golfer's tee.

I spy

two fangs,

 five yellow toes,

a paper clip mouth,

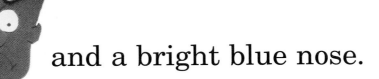 and a bright blue nose.

I spy

five dark bones,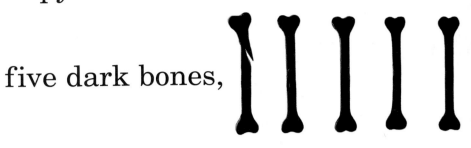

 a bat,

two musical notes,

 and a bell on a cat.

I spy

an anchor,

 a big horseshoe,

a door,

 and a ghost you can
see right through.

I spy  a fish,

two horns on a head,

 two green worms,

and a snake that's red.

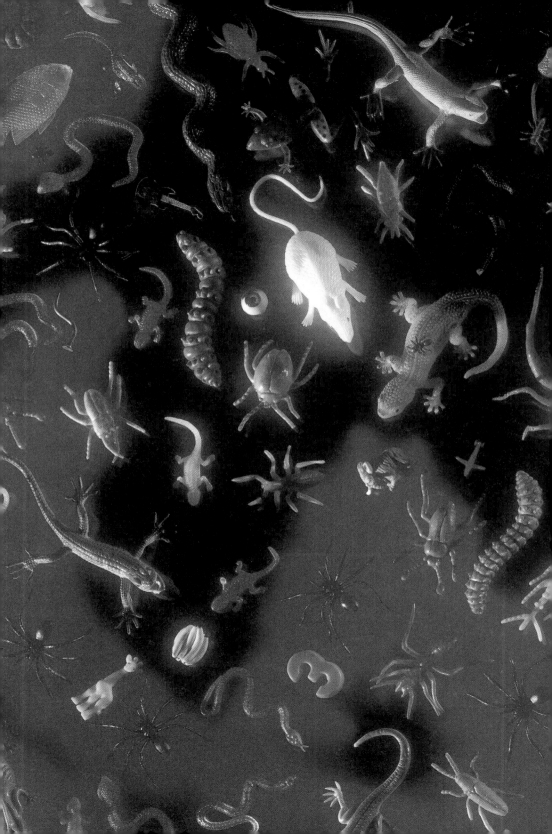

I spy

a cheetah,

 pants that are green,

a dog,

 and a mask for Halloween.

I spy

 a frog,

a hammer,

 a horse,

two dusty bones,

 and a skeleton, of course!

I spy two matching words.

 two green worms

a pumpkin

 pants that are green

I spy two matching words.

five yellow toes

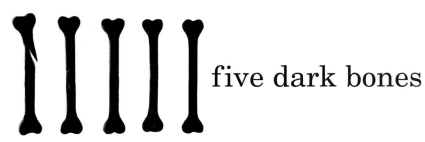 five dark bones

two fangs

I spy two words that start with the letter D.

a bell on a cat

 two dusty bones

door

I spy two words that start
with the letters SK.

skeleton

a snake that's red

smoky skull

I spy two words that end with the letters ER.

silver key

 a mask for Halloween

hammer

I spy two words that end with the letters GHT.

a ghost you can see right through

a bright blue nose

a paper clip mouth

I spy two words that rhyme.

 horn player's hat

a frog

bat

I spy two words that rhyme.

golfer's tee

 three golden eggs

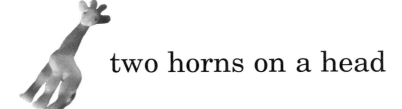 two horns on a head